Sylvie

Sylvie

GÉRARD DE NERVAL

Translated and with a preface by
RICHARD SIEBURTH

SYRENS

GÉRARD DE NERVAL 1808–1855

S Y R E N S Published by the Penguin Group. Penguin Books Ltd, 27 Wrights Lane, London W8 5TZ, England. Penguin Books USA Inc., 375 Hudson Street, New York, New York 10014, USA. Penguin Books Australia Ltd, Ringwood, Victoria, Australia. Penguin Books Canada Ltd, 10 Alcorn Avenue, Toronto, Ontario, Canada M4V 3B2. Penguin Books (NZ) Ltd, 182–190 Wairau Road, Auckland 10, New Zealand. Penguin Books Ltd, Registered Offices: Harmonds-worth, Middlesex, England. Published in Syrens 1995. Translation and preface copyright © Richard Sieburth, 1995. All rights reserved. The moral right of the translator has been asserted. Except in the United States of America, this book is sold subject to the condition that it shall not, by way of trade or otherwise, be lent, re-sold, hired out, or otherwise circulated without the publisher's prior consent in any form of binding or cover other than that in which it is published and without a similar condition including this condition being imposed on the subsequent purchaser. Set in 9.5/12 pt Monotype Bembo by Datix International Limited, Bungay, Suffolk. Printed and bound by Page Bros., Norwich.

1 2 3 4 5 6 7 8 9 10

Nerval wrote *Sylvie* during one of his last seasons of
serenity, a year and a half before his suicide, enjoying
a brief respite from what he called his 'black butter-
flies'. Released from the Paris clinic where he had
been hospitalized after one of his recurring episodes
of mental disarray, he spent the spring and summer
of 1853 convalescing, making periodic excursions on
foot through the woods and country lanes of the
nearby Valois, reacquainting himself with the vistas
of his childhood. Working somewhat like a painter –
the landscapes of *Sylvie* have often been compared to
those of Corot or the Impressionists – Nerval
sketched out his story in peripatetic fashion, jotting
down his random memories and meditations in

pencil on stray pieces of paper. But the subsequent weaving together of these scattered strands of reverie into the seamless mesh of his final text caused him, by his own accounts, considerable anguish. In late August, one week after the publication of his tale in *La Revue des Deux Mondes*, exhausted by his labours, suffering from persistent insomnia, he relapsed: he was confined to a private sanatorium in Passy, there to spend most of his remaining days.

'J'efface tout à mesure que j'écris,' Nerval confessed in one of his progress reports to his editor: the more he wrote, the more he seemed to cross out. Like Freud's Mystic Writing Pad (or Penelope's web, for that matter), *Sylvie* is a parable about the ravelling and unravelling of fictions, or more precisely, about the kind of ever-shifting palimpsest created by a memory engaged in the simultaneous pressures of recollection and repression, inscription and obliteration. Just as its narrator's present is constantly deleted or deferred by the traces impressed on it by the past, so, by an obverse mechanism, the various places and events he elegiacally evokes only seem to take on real life and tangibility once they have been cancelled by time. The final, unsettling revelation of the tale – a dénouement worthy of Poe's *Ligeia* – is thus emblematic of the looking-glass logic it has been elaborating all the while: only that which is dead truly exists, only that which has been forgotten is truly remembered, only in erasure does the true image of our desire take shape.

In a 1909 essay on *Sylvie*, drafted as he was about to embark on his own epic investigation into time lost and regained, Marcel Proust discerned in the condensed compass of Nerval's short novella the germ of his own *magnum opus* to come. Its opening pages, he could not fail to notice, adumbrated his own intuitions of the workings of involuntary memory: indeed, the whole plot of *Sylvie* is set into motion when the narrator's eye, by the purest of chance, happens to fall on a few lines in a newspaper announcing a local festival to be held the following day in the Valois. His memory startled from its slumbers by this insignificant piece of journalistic information – whose power (a point not lost on the future author of *A La Recherche*) lies precisely in its magic naming of *place* – he experiences that peculiarly Proustian moment of grace whereby the past unexpectedly resurrects itself as an imagined whole within the ruins of the present: a series of impressions or tableaux, as Nerval puts it, compressed into a single spot of time.

But this initial epiphany of *Sylvie*, far from being

redemptive (as it might have been for a Wordsworth or Chateaubriand) merely plunges its narrator further into the abyss of temporality. Unable to sleep, haunted by the images of the past called up by his fortuitous reading of this newspaper item, he sets off from Paris at one in the morning to make his way to the annual St Bartholomew's feastday at Loisy, a country village situated a mere twenty miles or so from the capital as the crow flies, but a destination that it will take him some four hours by night coach (and as many intervening chapters of flashbacks) eventually to reach. Like the celebrated ouverture to *Combray*, the first half of *Sylvie* places us within the particular gravitational warp of a consciousness experiencing a free-fall through space and time, half-waking, half-dreaming, visited by a succession of apparently disconnected memories that branch back through adolescence and childhood and sink into various strata buried in the Valois' legendary past: Rousseau's neo-classical Ermenonville, the Italianate Renaissance of Catherine de Medicis, the early Gothic of Châalis, the battle sites of the Romans and Gauls, the shadowy forest tribes of Sylvanects, the looming Druid rocks . . .

Proust observed that to read *Sylvie* for the first time was to experience a kind of disorientation verging on mild panic. Forced at every moment to leaf back the preceding pages just to get his textual bearings (particularly during the first seven nocturnal chapters of the story), the reader – like the narrator himself – feels lost in the woods, casting about for a few familiar landmarks that might allow him to fight his way free from the ever-encroaching thickets of the past and at last reach some sort of clearing, some sort of mappable vantage point in present space. But the sandy, marshy soil of Nerval's Valois – and in this it is not unlike Hardy's Wessex, Faulkner's Yoknapatawpha, or (again) Proust's Combray – offers little *terra firma*. *Sylvie* is not, as many nineteenth-century readers thought, a regionalist *roman champêtre* in the bucolic manner of George Sand, but rather, as Proust was the first to note, a ghost story, a Dostoyevskian tale of obsession disguised as a wistfully innocuous version of pastoral. Its *genius loci* is the twilight zone of the fantastic – that uncanny place where everything seems at once foreign and familiar, irretrievably lost and hauntingly present, not quite elsewhere, not quite here. We have yet to learn how to inhabit it.

Richard Sieburth

Sylvie

Memories of the Valois

1. *A Wasted Night*

I was coming out of a theatre where, night after night, I would appear in one of the stage boxes, dressed in the elegant garb of an ardent suitor. At times the place was full, at others empty. But it mattered little to me whether my gaze happened to fall on a parterre merely occupied by thirty or so hired enthusiasts or on balconies bedecked with hats and gowns long gone out of fashion – or whether I instead found myself part of an audience buzzing with excitement, every tier crowned with colourful corsages, glittering jewels and beaming faces. Not only was I indifferent to the spectacle provided by the audience, but the events on stage barely held my attention – except when, at the second or third scene of some dismal masterpiece of the day, a familiar vision would suddenly illuminate the vacant space and, with a single breath or word, infuse new life into the empty figures surrounding me on all sides.

I felt myself alive in her, and she lived for me alone. Her every smile filled me with infinite bliss; each quaver of her voice, so gentle and yet so profoundly resonant, sent shivers of joy and love through me. For me, she was utter perfection, an answer to my every rapture, my every whim. When she was lit from below by the footlights, she was as lovely as the day; and when the lights dimmed, showing her off more naturally beneath the rays of the chandelier overhead, she was as pale as the night, her sole beauty shining forth from the dark like those divine Hours who stand out so distinctly from the brown backgrounds of the frescoes at Hercula-neum, stars on their brows.[1]

For an entire year it had not even occurred to me to find out who or what she might really be; I was afraid to cloud the magic mirror that cast her image back at me. All that reached my ears was some

---

[1] In classical myth, the four Hours regulate the orderly procession of the seasons. Nerval had visited the excavations at Herculaneum while in Naples.

gossip pertaining to her not as an actress, but as a woman. But I paid no more attention to this talk than I would to rumours concerning the Princess of Elis or the Queen of Trebizond,[2] for one of my uncles who had lived through the penultimate years of the eighteenth century (and who knew the period as only those who had truly experienced it could) had warned me quite early on that actresses were not women, nature having forgotten to endow them with hearts. He was speaking of the actresses of his own day, no doubt; but he had told me so many stories about his illusions and disappointments, he had shown me so many portraits on ivory (lovely medallions with which he subsequently decorated his snuff boxes) and so many yellowed love letters and faded favours, while recounting the sad tales that went with each, that I became accustomed to think ill of all actresses, regardless of their place in time.

We were then living in a strange period, one of those eras that usually follow in the wake of revolutions or the declines of great reigns. But its hallmark was no longer the heroic gallantry of the Fronde, the

---

2 Heroines, respectively, of Molière's *La Princesse d'Élide* and of *La Princesse de Trébizonde*, a popular operetta of the early nineteenth century.

stylish vice of the Regency, or the scepticism and outlandish debauchery of the Directory.³ It was instead a mixture of activity, hesitation and indolence, an assortment of dazzling Utopias, religious or philosophic aspirations, vague enthusiasms and dim intimations of renaissance in which a general weariness with the discords of the past was blended with ill-defined hopes for the future – a period, in short, not unlike the age in which Peregrinus or Apuleius lived.⁴ Material man longed for the bouquet of roses which would regenerate him at the hands of the lovely Isis; forever young, forever pure, the goddess would appear to us at night, filling us with shame for having so wasted the hours of the day.⁵ Worldly ambitions, however, meant little to our generation; the greedy scramble for honours and positions in

3 The Fronde (1648–53), the Regency (1710–23), the Directory (1795–9).
4 The second-century philosophers Peregrinus and Apuleius were noted for the unstable syncretism of their doctrines. Nerval rhymes their era of imperial decline with the aftermath of the July Revolution of 1830.
5 Metamorphosed into an ass, Lucius, the hero of Apuleius' romance *The Golden Ass*, is in the end physically and spiritually rehumanized when he eats the roses strewn by the celebrants of the Eleusinian cult of Isis.

which everybody was then engaged only served to distance us from all possible spheres of activity. The sole refuge left to us was the poets' ivory tower – which we climbed, higher and higher, in order to isolate ourselves from the crowd. Having been guided to these heights by our masters, we at last breathed the pure air of solitude, drinking ourselves into oblivion from the golden cup of fable, drunk with poetry and love – love, alas, of vague shapes, of blue and rosy hues, of metaphysical phantoms. Seen close, any real woman seemed too gross to our starry-eyed sensibilities. She had to appear a queen or goddess: above all, she had to lie beyond reach.

Some of us, however, were not too keen on these Platonic paradoxes, and amid our renewed fantasies of Alexandria, we would occasionally brandish the torch of the gods of the underworld, momentarily illuminating the darkness with a trail of sparks. Thus it was that when I emerged from the theatre, bitterly mourning my vanished dreams, I was eager to make my way to a club where a good number of us used to sup and where all traces of melancholy would be dissipated by the boundless vitality of the various brilliant wits who gathered there. Wits such as these – lively, unpredictable, occasionally sublime – are an inevitable feature of periods of renewal or decline, and sometimes their discussions reached such a pitch that the more timid among us would now and then go to the windows to see whether the Huns, the Turkomans or the Cossacks were not knocking at the gates to cut short the sheer rhetoric and sophistry of these arguments.

'You can't go wrong with wine, women and song!' Such, at least, was the opinion of the younger members of the club. One of them said to me: 'I keep seeing you at the same theatre these days. So *who* is she?'

Who? ... Somehow, I couldn't imagine going there for anyone *else*. But I let her name slip out none the less. 'Well,' said my friend with sympathy, 'if you look over there you'll see the lucky fellow who has just escorted her home and who, faithful to the laws of our club, will probably not rejoin her till night is passed.'

Casually, I looked over at the person in question. He was young, well-dressed, with a pale, nervous face, excellent manners and a gentle, melancholy gaze. He was tossing sums of gold on to a whist table and seemed indifferent to the amount he was losing. 'What difference should it make', I said to myself, 'if it is this person or another? There was bound to be someone, and this fellow seems worthy of her choice.'

'And you?'

'Me? I'm chasing after an image, nothing more.'

On my way out, as I was passing through the reading-room, I absent-mindedly glanced at one of the newspapers. I think it was because I wanted to see how the stock market was faring. Among the various assets that had not yet slipped through my fingers, there was a fairly substantial batch of foreign securities. There had been a rumour that these securities, which had long been deemed worthless, were about to be formally recognized – and indeed, after a government reshuffle, this is precisely what had just taken place. Their market value had already risen considerably; I was a rich man again!

The first thing that came to my mind after this change of fortunes was that the woman I had so long adored was now mine for the asking. My ideal was henceforth within reach. But how could I be sure I was not merely the victim of yet one more illusion, the dupe of some cruel misprint? Yet the facts were confirmed by all the other newspapers. The sum I had just gained loomed before me like some golden effigy of Moloch. I thought to myself, 'What would that young fellow over there say if I were to go and take his place beside the woman whom he has left all alone . . .' I shuddered at the thought; it was beneath my pride.

No! I'm not about to kill love with gold at my age: I refuse to play the corrupter. Besides, this is no longer the way one goes about things these days. Where did I get the idea that this woman might be swayed by money? As I vaguely ran my eye over the newspaper I was still holding in my hands, my attention was caught by these two lines: '*Fête du Bouquet provincial* – Tomorrow the archers of Senlis will present the bouquet to the archers of Loisy.' These few simple words awoke a whole new series of impressions in my mind: they brought back a memory of country life I had long forgotten, a distant echo of the innocent festivals of my youth. The far-off sound of drum and horn was drifting through the hamlets and woods; the young girls were weaving garlands and tying ribbons around bouquets, singing all the while. A heavy wagon, drawn by oxen, was receiving these offerings as it passed; and we, the children of these parts, were escorting it with our bows and arrows, imagining ourselves knights of old – unaware that we were merely repeating from age to age a Druidic festival that had survived all subsequent monarchies and forms of religion.

II. *Adrienne*

I went home to bed but could not rest. As I lay there in a half-sleep, my entire youth passed through my memory. This state, in which the mind is still fending off the bizarre concatenations of dream, often allows one to see the most salient tableaux of an extended period of life compressed into a few minutes.

In my mind's eye I saw a castle from the days of Henri IV with its pointed, slate-covered roofs, its reddish façade notched by yellow quoins, its great green lawn framed by elms and limes, their leaves shot through with the fiery shafts of the setting sun. Young girls were doing a round dance on the lawn, singing old melodies handed down to them by their mothers; their French, so naturally pure, left no doubt as to the location – that ancient land of Valois where, for more than a thousand years, the heart of France has beaten.

I was the only boy in the round, and I had brought along my young little friend, Sylvie, a girl from the neighbouring village, so fresh, so full of life, with her dark eyes, her regular profile and her lightly tanned skin! . . . She was my only love, I had eyes only for her – that is, up to that moment! In the round we were dancing, I had barely noticed the tall, beautiful fair-haired girl by the name of Adrienne. As the rules of the dance would have it, Adrienne suddenly found herself alone by my side in the middle of the circle. We were the same height. We were told to kiss, and the dancing and the singing whirled around us ever more swiftly. As I kissed her I could not resist giving her hand a squeeze. The long, tight ringlets of her golden hair grazed my cheeks. From that moment onward, I was overcome by an inner turmoil unfamiliar to me. In order to be allowed to resume her place in the dance, the beautiful girl was required to sing a song. Everybody sat down around her, and in a voice that was at once fresh, piercing and yet slightly gauzy (like the voices of so many of the girls in this land of mists), she proceeded to sing one of those old ballads, full of melancholy and love, which inevitably tell of the misfortunes of some princess who has been locked away in a tower by her father as a punishment for having fallen in love. At the end of every stanza, the melody trailed off into one of those wavering trills which young voices know how to produce so effectively whenever they modulate their tremolo in imitation of the quavering voices of their grandmothers.

As she sang, the shadows came down from the

great trees and she stood there alone, lit by the first rays of the moon, set apart from our attentive circle. She stopped singing, and no one dared break the silence. Thin clouds of mist drifted over the lawn, spreading tufts of white upon the tips of the grass. We thought we were in paradise. Finally, I got up and ran over to the castle gardens where there were laurels planted in huge faïence vases painted in monochrome. I brought back two branches which were twined into a crown and tied with a ribbon. I placed this wreath on Adrienne's head; the glossy leaves upon her fair hair gleamed in the pale rays of the moon. She resembled Dante's Beatrice, smiling upon the poet as he wandered at the outer reaches of her blessèd abode.

Adrienne rose. As her slender figure slipped away, she made a gracious bow in our direction and ran back towards the castle. It was said she was the grandchild of one of the descendants of a family allied to the ancient kings of France; the blood of the house of Valois coursed in her veins. On this particular holiday, she had been allowed to mingle in our games; but we were never to see her again, for the following day she returned to the convent where she was a boarder.

When I returned to Sylvie's side, I noticed she was

crying. The crown I had conferred upon the lovely singer with my own hands was the reason for her tears. I offered to go and gather more laurels for her, but she said it didn't matter, since she hardly deserved a crown. I tried in vain to mollify her, she did not utter a single word as I escorted her back home.

Obliged to return to Paris to resume my studies, I carried a double image away with me – of a tender friendship that had sadly gone awry and of a love at once impossible and ill-defined, a source of aching thoughts which no amount of schoolroom philosophy could allay.

It was the sole figure of Adrienne that triumphed in the end – a mirage of glory and beauty whose company sweetened my hours of strenuous schoolwork. The following year, during the holidays, I learned that this lovely girl whom I had scarcely glimpsed had been placed in a nunnery by her family.

III. *Resolution*

To me, this half-dreamt memory explained everything. This vague, hopeless love I had conceived for an actress, this love which swept me up every evening when the curtain rose, only to release me when sleep finally descended, had its seed in the memory of Adrienne, a night-flower blooming in the pale effulgence of the moon, a phantom fair and rosy gliding over the green grass half-bathed in white mist. This resemblance to a figure I had long forgotten was now taking shape with singular vividness; it was a pencil sketch smudged by time that was now turning into a painting, like those studies by the Old Masters that one has admired in some museum, only to discover their dazzling original somewhere else.

To be in love with a nun in the guise of an actress! . . . and what if they were one and the same! It is enough to drive one mad – the fatal lure of the unknown drawing one ever onward like a will o' the wisp flitting over the rushes of a stagnant pool . . . Let us try to regain our grip on reality . . .

And Sylvie whom I so loved, why have I forgotten her these past three years? . . . She was a very lovely girl, the loveliest in Loisy!

She does exist, this girl, still good and pure of heart no doubt. I can still see her window with its rosebush intertwined with vines and its cage of linnets hanging to the left; I can hear the clicking of her lace bobbins and the strains of her favourite song:

> The lovely maid was sitting
> By the rushing stream . . .

She is still waiting for me . . . Poor as she is, who would have married her?

In her village and those surrounding it, solid peasants in smocks, with leathery hands, gaunt faces and weathered skins. But I was her true love, I, the little Parisian who used to come out to Loisy to visit my poor uncle near by, now deceased. For the past three years, living like a prince, I have been frittering away the modest inheritance he left me and which might have lasted me an entire life. With Sylvie, I would have held on to it. Now, by a stroke of luck, I've recouped some of my fortune. There is still time.

What would she be doing at this hour? Sleeping . . . No, she's not sleeping; today they are celebrating the Festival of the Bow, the only holiday in the entire year where one dances the whole night through. She must be taking part in the festivities . . .

What time is it?

I was without a watch.

Amid the bric-à-brac which it was then customary to collect in order to restore the period flavour of ancient apartments, there was one of those Renaissance tortoiseshell pendulum-clocks, buffed back to its original sheen, whose gilded dome, surmounted by a figure of Time, is supported by caryatids in the Medici style, resting in their turn on half-rearing horses. The historical Diana leaning on her stag appears in low relief below the face on which the enamelled numbers of the hours stand out against an inlaid background. The works, no doubt still serviceable, had not been wound in two centuries. But then, it was not to tell time that I had purchased this clock in Touraine.

I went downstairs to the porter's lodge. The cuckoo clock indicated it was one in the morning. Within four hours, I said to myself, I could be at the Loisy ball. Out on the square of the Palais-Royal, there were still five or six cabs waiting for customers from the nearby clubs and gambling houses.

'Take me to Loisy!' I said to the first one I saw.

'Where's that?'

'Near Senlis, it's about twenty miles.'

'I'll drop you off at the coach station,' said the driver who had less on his mind than I did.

What a dreary drive the road to Flanders is at night; things only start looking more attractive once you get into the forested areas. To either side, there is the same endless file of trees coming at you with their vague, twisted shapes. And beyond this, squares of green fields or plots of ploughed earth bounded to the left by the bluish hills of Montmorency, Ecouen and Luzarches. Here is Gonesse, a vulgar little town full of memories of the Ligue[6] and the Fronde.

Beyond Louvres there is a lane lined with apple trees whose flowers I have often seen glimmer in the night like the stars above – it was a short cut to the backwoods villages. While the coach is making its way up the hills, let us piece together the memories of the days when I often visited these parts.

IV. *A Voyage to Cythera*

Some years had lapsed: my meeting with Adrienne in front of the castle had already become no more than a childhood memory. I happened to be in Loisy for the annual parish feast. I once again joined the Knights of the Bow, taking my place within their ranks as on former occasions. The festivities had

6 Roman Catholic organization formed in the late sixteenth century to combat Protestantism.

been organized by some of the young descendants of the various old families who still own the sundry castles scattered throughout the forests of the region, more battered by time than by revolutions. Streaming in from Chantilly, Compiègne and Senlis, bands of revellers were joining into the rustic procession of the Companies of the Bow. After the long parade through the villages and hamlets, after mass in church, after the archery contests and the awarding of prizes, the victors had been invited to a banquet which was to take place on an isle shaded by limes and poplars in the middle of one of the lakes fed by the rivers Nonette and Thève. Small boats, all decked out with flags, ferried us over to the island – the site had been chosen because it featured an oval temple with columns which was going to serve as the banquet hall. Here, as at Ermenonville, the countryside is dotted with airy constructions dating back to the end of the eighteenth century, when millionaire free-thinkers drew their architectural inspirations from the reigning fashions of the day. I believe that this particular temple had originally been dedicated to Urania. Three of its columns had collapsed, carrying along with them a portion of the architrave; but the interior had been cleared of debris and garlands had been strung between the columns, thus rejuvenating this modern ruin – a remnant of the paganism of

Boufflers or Chaulieu rather than that of Horace.[7]

The crossing of the lake had perhaps been devised to recall Watteau's *Voyage to Cythera*. Our modern dress alone spoiled the illusion. The huge festal bouquet had been removed from its wagon and placed on a large boat; the cortège of young girls all clad in white who, according to custom, provided its escort, had taken their seats in the boat, and this graceful *theory*, reviving the days of antiquity, was reflected in the calm waters of the lake as it made its way towards the banks of the island which lay beyond, its thickets of hawthorn, its colonnades and lambent leaves tinged bright red by the setting sun. All the boats soon reached shore. The ceremonial basket of flowers occupied the centre of the table, and each guest took his place; the most favoured ones were seated next to the girls: to enjoy this privilege it was enough to be a family acquaintance. It was thus that I found myself next to Sylvie. Her brother had already come up to me during the festivities and reproached me for not having paid a

7 Two minor eighteenth-century poets whose rococo neo-classicism recalls that of Watteau, a painter largely forgotten in the nineteenth century until rediscovered by Nerval and his circle in the 1830s.

visit to his family in a long while. I offered as an excuse that my studies had kept me in Paris, and assured him that I had returned with precisely this in mind. 'No, I'm the one he has forgotten,' said Sylvie. 'We're just country bumpkins, too lowly for a Parisian!' I wanted to kiss her words away, but she was still sulking, and it took her brother's intervention to get her to offer me her cheek with an air of indifference. I took no pleasure in this kiss of hers which she accorded to me as if I were nobody in particular, for in this bucolic region where greetings are exchanged with every passerby, a kiss is nothing more than a polite gesture between honest folk.

The organizers of the feast had come up with a surprise. At the close of the banquet, a wild swan, hitherto held captive under the flowers, struggled free from the tangle of garlands and chaplets and managed to scatter them in all directions with its powerful wings. As it soared forth in joy into the last glimmers of the sun, each of us snatched up a stray chaplet and immediately proceeded to crown his neighbour. I was fortunate enough to have caught one of the loveliest ones and Sylvie, now all smiles, allowed me to kiss her far more tenderly than before. I understood that I was thereby effacing the memory of an earlier occasion. This time, my admiration for her was undivided, she had become so beautiful! She was no longer that little village girl whom I had scorned for someone grander and more worldly in her graces. She had improved in every respect: the lure of her dark eyes, so seductive even as a child, had become irresistible; beneath the arcs of her eyebrows, her smile, suddenly brightening the regularity and serenity of her countenance, had something Athenian to it. Compared to the pleasant but somewhat lopsided features of her companions, I found her face worthy of the art of antiquity. Her delicately tapered hands, the white contours of her arms, the ease with which she carried herself – all made her a creature quite different from the girl I had known. I could not help commenting on how changed I found her, hoping thereby to cover over my former fleeting infidelity.

Besides, everything was in my favour: her brother's friendship, the enchanting effect of these festivities, the evening hour and the very place itself – where, by a tasteful feat of fancy, the image of the stately gallantries of times gone by had been reproduced. At every opportunity, we slipped off from the dance to talk of our childhood memories and to admire the reflections of the sky on the waters and shadowy groves, lost in a common dream. It was

Sylvie's brother who finally broke the spell, inform-
ing us that it was time to make the long journey
home to their family's village.

v. *The Village*

They lived in Loisy, in the old gamekeeper's lodge. I
accompanied them there, then returned to Montagny[8] where I was staying at my uncle's. Leaving
the road to cut across the woods that separate Loisy
from Saint-S . . ., I soon found myself wandering
along the sunken path that skirts the forest of Ermenonville; I was expecting at any moment to come
across the walls of a convent which I would then
have to follow for about a mile. From time to time
the moon would slip behind the clouds, barely illuminating the dark granite rocks and the ever-increasing
tufts of broom underfoot. To the right and to the
left, the fringe of the trackless forests, and before me,
endless Druidic rock-formations still harbouring the

8 A name that screens Mortefontaine, the village in which the
motherless Gérard Labrunie (Nerval's real name) spent his early
childhood years in the care of relatives. His mother's family owned
a nearby paddock known as the 'clos de Nerval'.

local memory of the sons of Armen exterminated by the Romans. From the heights of these sublime agglomerations, I gazed upon the distant lakes which flashed like mirrors against the misty plain, but was unable to distinguish which one had been the site of the festivities.

The air was balmy; I decided to venture no further and to await the morning, so I lay down on some tufts of broom. When I woke up, I gradually recognized the various landmarks near the area where I had lost my bearings the previous night. To my left, I saw the walls of the convent of Saint-S... stretching off in a long line, and to the other side of the valley, the Butte aux Gens-d'Armes with the shattered ruins of an ancient Carlovingian palace. In the same vicinity, visible above the clumps of trees, the great tumbledown walls of the abbey of Thiers, pierced with trefoils and ogees, were outlined against the horizon. Beyond this, the Gothic manor-house of Pontarmé, still surrounded by water as in ancient times, was now reflecting the first fires of day, while to the south, the tall keep of La Tournelle and the four towers of Bertrand-Fosse rose on the front ranges of Montméliant.

I had passed a delightful night, and Sylvie was the

only thing on my mind; none the less, at the sight of the convent, it momentarily occurred to me that this was perhaps where Adrienne lived. The matin bells were still ringing in my ears; it was this, no doubt, which had awoken me. It occurred to me that by climbing to the highest point of the rock-formation, I might get a glimpse over the walls; but, on second thoughts, I shrank back from the idea, for it struck me as a profanation. As dawn grew into day, it chased this vain memory from my mind; only the rosy features of Sylvie remained. 'Let's go and wake her up,' I said to myself, and I made my way to Loisy.

Here, at the end of the trail that skirts the forest, lies the village: twenty cottages with walls garlanded with vines and climbing roses. Gathered in front of a farm, wearing red kerchiefs on their heads, a group of women is already at work spinning. Sylvie is not among them. Ever since she started making fine lace, she has become quite the young lady, whereas her relatives have remained mere village folk. I went up to her room without creating any surprise; she had already been up for some time and was working on a piece of lace, her bobbins softly clicking away on the green cushion she held on her knees. 'Here you are, lazy bones,' she said with her divine smile;

'You've probably just got out of bed.' I told her of my sleepless night, of how I had wandered this way and that among the woods and rocks. She was kind enough to take pity on me for a moment. 'If you're not too worn out, I'll help you stretch your legs a bit more. We'll go and visit my great aunt at Othys.' I barely had time to reply; she leapt to her feet excitedly, arranged her hair in the mirror, and put on a rustic straw hat. Her eyes sparkled with joy and innocence. We set off along the banks of the Thève, across meadows strewn with daisies and buttercups, then skirted the woods of Saint-Laurent, taking short cuts across the occasional stream or thicket. The thrushes warbled in the trees and the tits darted playfully from the bushes we grazed as we walked along.

Every now and then we would come across one of those periwinkles of which Rousseau was so fond, their blue corollas opening amid the intertwined boughs whose long trains kept tripping up my companion's light feet. Indifferent to the memory of the Genevan philosopher, she gathered fragrant strawberries here and there while I spoke to her of *La Nouvelle Héloïse*, reciting passages from it by heart.

'Is it pretty?' she asked.

'It's sublime.'

'Is it better than Auguste Lafontaine?'[9]

'It's more tender.'

'Well,' she said, 'I'll have to read it then. I'll ask my brother to bring me back a copy the next time he goes to Senlis.' And I continued to recite fragments of the *Héloïse* while Sylvie picked strawberries.

VI. *Othys*

On emerging from the woods, we came upon large bunches of purple foxglove; she gathered them into an enormous bouquet, saying: 'They're for my aunt; she'll be so happy to have these lovely flowers in her room.' There was just a slight stretch of open country cover before reaching Othys. The village spire was already visible on the bluish hills that extend from Montméliant to Dammartin. The Thève was once again burbling over rocks and pebbles as it dwindled to a narrow stream near its source – where it rests among the meadows, forming a small pond amid irises and gladiolas. We soon reached the

9 Early nineteenth-century German author of sentimental pastoral romances.

outskirts of the village. Sylvie's aunt lived in a small cottage built of uneven granite fieldstones and covered with trellises of hop and honeysuckle. She lived alone on some plots of land which her fellow villagers cultivated for her after her husband's death. The arrival of her niece caused quite a stir. 'Good morning, aunt! Your children are here!' said Sylvie. 'And are we hungry!' She kissed her tenderly, pressed the bouquet into her arms, and then, at last remembering to introduce me, said: 'This is my sweetheart!'

I in turn kissed her aunt. She said: 'What a nice young fellow . . . So he's a blond . . .'

'He has a fine head of hair,' said Sylvie.

'Which won't last long,' said her aunt. 'But you both have time ahead of you, and your dark locks go very nicely with his.'

'Aunt, let's get him something to eat,' said Sylvie. And she went into the cupboards and the pantry and found some milk, some brown bread and some sugar, and casually set the table with a few earthenware dishes and platters decorated with large flowers and brightly plumed cockerels. A Creil porcelain tureen, filled with strawberries floating in milk, provided the centrepiece, and having filched a few handfuls of cherries and gooseberries from the garden, she placed a vase of flowers at either end of the tablecloth. Her aunt, however, rather aptly remarked: 'All this is merely dessert. You leave things up to me now.' And she took the frying pan down from its peg and threw a log on the tall hearth. 'Don't you lay a hand on it!' she said to Sylvie, who was anxious to help out. 'Imagine ruining those pretty fingers that make lace that's even finer than the work they do at Chantilly! You've given me some of your handiwork, so I know what I'm talking about.'

'Of course you do, aunt! . . . You wouldn't have any old bits of lace lying around, would you? I could use them as patterns.'

'Well, you might have a look upstairs,' said her aunt. 'There may be some in my chest of drawers.'

'Give me the keys,' Sylvie said.

'Nonsense,' said her aunt, 'I never lock the drawers.'

'That's not true, there's one drawer you always keep locked.' And while the old lady was wiping the frying pan clean after having warmed it over the fire, Sylvie undid her apron-strings and removed a little key of wrought steel and held it up to me in triumph.

I quickly followed her up the wooden stairs that led to the bedroom. Oh the holiness of youth and old age! Who would have thought of sullying the purity of a first love in this sanctuary of faithful memories? The dark eyes and rosy lips of a young man of yesteryear were smiling from an oval, gilt-framed portrait that hung at the head of the rustic bed. He was wearing the uniform of the gamekeepers of the house of Condé; his more or less martial pose, his rosy, good-humoured looks, the candour of his brow beneath his powdered hair, imparted an aura of youth and simplicity to this no doubt mediocre pastel. Some modest artist, invited to join the prince's hunting parties, had tried his best to *limn* the young gamekeeper and his bride, who was to be seen in another medallion, comely, mischievous, slender in her open bodice laced with ribbons, her lips puckered as she teased a bird perched on her finger. It was in fact the same old lady who was at that very moment downstairs cooking, stooped over the hearth. I was reminded of the pantomimes at the Funambules,[10] where the fairies would hide behind wrinkled masks, only to reveal their lovely faces at the dénouement, when the temple of Love made its appearance in a nimbus of magical rays cast by its whirling sun. 'Oh how pretty you were, dear aunt!' I exclaimed.

'And me?' said Sylvie, who had managed to get

10 Popular Parisian theatre whose speciality was pantomime.

the drawer open. She had found a flowing gown of shot silk whose every fold rustled at her touch. 'Let me try it on to see if it suits me,' she said. 'It will probably make me look like an old fairy.'

'Like the fairy of legend blessed with eternal youth! . . .' I murmured to myself. Sylvie had already undone her calico dress and let it slip to her feet. Her old aunt's taffeta gown fitted her slim figure perfectly, and she asked me to fasten it for her.

'These sleeves are ridiculous,' she said. And yet the lace-trimmed puffs showed off her bare arms to great advantage, and her bust was nicely framed by the yellowed tulle and faded ribbons of the bodice which had scarcely encased the vanished charms of her aunt. 'Stop fumbling around! Don't you know how to hook a dress?' said Sylvie. She looked the very picture of Greuze's *Village Bride*.

'We'll need some powder,' I said. 'We're sure to find some.' She rummaged around some more in the drawers. What a treasure trove! How sweetly it all smelled, how the cheap trinkets and bright colours all glittered and gleamed! Two mother-of-pearl fans that were slightly damaged, pasteboard boxes with Chinese motifs, an amber necklace and myriad other trifles, among which two small white felt shoes with buckles incrusted with imitation diamonds.

'Oh, let me put them on,' said Sylvie. 'Let's see if we can find the embroidered stockings that go with them.'

A minute later, we were unrolling some pale pink stockings with green figure-work about the ankles; but her aunt's voice and the sizzling of the frying pan suddenly called us back to reality. 'Hurry down!' said Sylvie, and despite my protests, she would not allow me to help her on with her shoes and stockings. Meanwhile, her aunt had just transferred the contents of the pan on to a platter, a slice of fried bacon and some eggs. But Sylvie's voice called me back upstairs. 'Quick, you get dressed too!' she said, and now entirely costumed herself, she showed me the game-keeper's wedding outfit laid out on the chest of drawers. In an instant, I was transformed into a bridegroom of another century. Sylvie was waiting for me on the landing, and the two of us proceeded down the stairs hand in hand. The aunt uttered a cry as she turned around and saw us: 'Oh, my children,' she exclaimed, and began to weep, then smiled through her tears. It was the image of her youth – a cruel and charming apparition. We took our seats by her side, quite moved and almost solemn, then we all grew light-hearted again when, the first shock passed, the old lady began regaling us with memories of her elaborate wedding. She even managed to recall some of the songs which it was the custom in those days to sing back and forth across the banquet table, just as she remembered the quaint epithalamium which had accompanied the newlyweds as they returned home from the dancing. We sang along with these stanzas, with their simple rhymes and their bygone assonances and hiatuses – as flowery and as impassioned as the Song of Songs. We were bride and bridegroom one whole, fine summer morn.

VII. *Châalis*

It is four o'clock in the morning; the road dips into a fold in the terrain, then rises again. The carriage will pass through Orry, then La Chapelle. To the left is a road that runs along the woods of Hallate. This is the road Sylvie's brother took the evening he drove me over to some local celebration in his dogcart. It was, I believe, the evening of the feast of Saint Bartholomew. His little horse flew through the woods along the back roads as if racing to a witches' sabbath. At Mont-Lévêque, we were back on cobblestones again and, several minutes later, we pulled up at the keeper's lodge at the ancient abbey of Châalis – Châalis, another memory of the past!

This ancient retreat of emperors no longer offers anything to the admiring eye except the ruins of its cloister with its Byzantine arcades, the last remnants of which are outlined against the pools – forgotten remains of those many pious foundations scattered through this area traditionally known as Charlemagne's 'smallholdings'. In this region, isolated from the bustle of cities and high roads, religion has retained some of the specific features imprinted on it by the cardinals of the House of Este over the course of their long residence here during the reign of the Medicis. Its various trappings and practices still have something quite gallant and poetic about them; the Renaissance still breathes beneath the delicately ribbed arches of chapels decorated by Italian artists. The rosy figures of saints and angels are profiled against the pale blue of the vaults, their allegorical pagan demeanour evoking the sensibility of a Petrarch or the mythical mysticism of a Francesco Colonna.[11]

---

11 Venetian author of *Polyphili Hypnerotomachia* (1499), a neo-Platonic allegory of the mystical love inspired by a female figure glimpsed in dreams.

We were intruders, Sylvie's brother and I, into the private festivities which were being held that evening. A person of illustrious birth, the current proprietor of this estate, had had the idea of inviting several of the region's families to attend a kind of allegorical dramatic presentation in which several boarders from a nearby convent were to perform. It was not a throwback to the tragedies played at Saint-Cyr;[12] it reached further back in time to the lyric dramas initially imported into France during the reigns of the Valois. What I saw performed was a mystery play from the days of old. The costumes, which consisted of long robes, varied only in their colour – azure, hyacinth, dawn. The action took place among the angels, amidst the debris of the devastated earth. Each voice sang in turn of the various splendours of this vanished world, and the angel of death spelled out the causes of its destruction. A spirit rose from the abyss, holding a flaming sword in its hand, and summoned the others to come and admire the glory of Christ, vanquisher of hell. The spirit was Adrienne, transfigured by her

12 School for the daughters of impoverished noblemen founded by Louis XIV and Mme de Maintenon; Racine's late Christian tragedies *Esther* and *Athalie* were first performed here.

costume, as she already was by her vocation. The halo of gilt cardboard around her angelic head seemed to us, quite naturally, a circle of light; her voice had gained in power and range, its every birdlike warble embroidering the phrases of a stately recitative with the infinite filigree of Italian song.

As I retrace these details, I tend to wonder if they are real or if I have dreamt them. Sylvie's brother was a bit tipsy that evening. We had stopped off for a few minutes in the keeper's lodge where – and this impressed me greatly – outside, there was a swan splayed upon the door and, inside, tall armoires of carved walnut, a large encased clock and various bows and arrows mounted as trophies above a red and green shooting target. A strange dwarf, wearing a Chinese cap, holding a bottle in one hand and a ring in the other, seemed to be inviting the archers to take their aim. The dwarf I believe was cut out of sheet-iron. But is the vision of Adrienne as real as these details or the incontrovertible existence of the abbey of Châalis? And yet it was surely the keeper's son who had ushered us into the hall where the performance was taking place; we stood by the door, at the back of a large audience which was solemnly sitting there, deeply moved. It was Saint Bartholomew's Day – a day singularly associated

with the memory of the Medicis whose arms, con-
joined with those of the House of Este, decorated
these ancient walls ... Perhaps this memory is an
obsession? Luckily the carriage is just now coming
to a stop on the route to Plessis; I am escaping from
the world of reverie and have but a quarter hour's
walk along the back roads before I reach Loisy.

VIII. *The Ball at Loisy*

I made my way into the ball at Loisy at that melancholy yet gentle hour when the lights all fade and
flicker at the approach of day. The lime-trees, still
dark below, were turning shades of blue at the top.
The village flute had ceased vying with the nightin-
gale's trills. Everybody was wan, and I had difficulty
recognizing any familiar faces among the groups
scattered here and there. Finally I caught sight of tall
Lise, a friend of Sylvie's. She greeted me with a kiss.
'We haven't seen you around in a long time, you
Parisian!' she said.

  'Yes, it's been a long time.'

  'And you've only just arrived.'

  'By coach.'

  'And none too soon!'

'I wanted to see Sylvie; is she still at the ball?'

'She never leaves before dawn; she just loves to dance.'

A minute later, I was by her side. Her features were drawn; but her dark eyes still sparkled with her former Athenian smile. A young man stood next to her. She motioned to him that she was going to sit out the next quadrille. He withdrew with a bow.

Day was breaking. We left the ball, hand in hand. The flowers in Sylvie's loosened hair were somewhat askew; and petals from her corsage were sprinkled on her rumpled lace, the skilful work of her own hands. I offered to escort her home. It was already broad day, but the sky was overcast. The Thève was burbling to our left; at each bend, it left behind pools of still water bespread with white and yellow lily pads, besprinkled with star grasses whose frail embroidery shimmered like daisies. Swathes and ricks of new-mown hay lay in the fields; the smell went to my head, but it lacked that power of intoxication which the fresh scent of the woods and hawthorn bushes used to harbour for me so long ago.

We had no thought of crossing these fields once more. 'Sylvie,' I said to her, 'you no longer love me!'

She heaved a sigh. 'My friend,' she said, 'one has to

accept things; life doesn't always turn out the way we want. You once spoke to me about *La Nouvelle Héloïse*, well I read it and I trembled when I saw its opening sentence: "Every young girl who reads this book is lost." And yet I forged onward, relying on my good judgment. Do you remember the day we dressed up in my aunt's wedding clothes? . . . The book's illustrations also depicted the lovers in old-fashioned dress, so that for me you were Saint-Preux and in Julie I recognized myself. Ah! If only you had come back again! But you were in Italy, so it was said. You must have seen far prettier girls there!'

'Sylvie, not a single one could match your eyes or the purity of your features. You may not know it, but you are a classical nymph. Besides, the woods of this region are as beautiful as those of the Roman Campagna. There are granite formations here that are no less sublime, and a waterfall that cascades down the rocks just like the one at Terni. I saw nothing there that I might regret here.'

'And in Paris?' she asked. 'In Paris . . .'

I shook my head without replying.

All of a sudden I thought of the vain image that had so long led me astray.

'Sylvie,' I said, 'why don't we stop here for a moment?'

I threw myself at her feet; dissolving into tears, I confessed my irresoluteness, my sudden changes of heart; I mentioned the fatal spectre that was plaguing my life.

'Save me!' I added. 'I'm coming back to you for good.'

She cast me a tender look . . .

At that very moment, our conversation was interrupted by hearty peals of laughter. It was Sylvie's brother joining us, bubbling over with high spirits, the inevitable result of a night of good country fun, considerably helped along by copious refreshments. He called over the beau of the ball, who was lagging behind, lost in the hawthorn thickets, and who soon caught up with us. This fellow was no more steady on his feet than his companion; he seemed even more embarrassed by the presence of a Parisian than by Sylvie's. His forthright face and embarrassed deference made it impossible for me to resent him for having been the dance partner who had caused her to stay on at the ball so late. I did not consider him much of a threat.

'We have to head home,' Sylvie said to her brother. 'See you later!' she said to me, offering her cheek.

Her sweetheart took no offence.

IX. *Ermenonville*

I had no desire to sleep. I went to Montagny to see
my uncle's house again. I was seized by great sadness
the moment I saw its yellow façade and green shutters. Everything seemed to be in its former state,
except that one had to go over to the farmer's
to get the front door key. Once the shutters were
open, I was moved to see that the furniture had been
kept in its same old condition, and was even polished
every now and then: the tall walnut cupboard, two
Flemish canvases, said to be the work of an ancient
painter, an ancestor of ours; some large engravings
after Boucher, and an entire series of framed illustrations to *Émile* and *La Nouvelle Héloïse* by Moreau; on
the table, a stuffed dog whom I had known alive and
who used to accompany me on my wanderings
through the woods, the last of the pugs, perhaps, for
he belonged to that lost breed.

'As for the parrot,' said the farmer, 'he's still alive;
I moved him to my place.'

The garden was a perfect picture of vegetation
run wild. In one of its corners, I recognized the
child's garden I had laid out there so long ago. A
shiver ran through me when I entered the study.

Everything was still in place: the small library of select books, lifelong friends of the deceased, as well as the desk with the various ancient relics he had dug up in his garden, some vases, some Roman medals, a collection of local finds that had been his pride and joy.

'Let's go and see the parrot,' I said to the farmer. The parrot was still calling for its food as it had in its better days and it looked at me, its round eye rimmed with wrinkled skin recalling the world-weary gaze of an old man.

Filled with the melancholy thoughts brought on by this belated return to such beloved scenes, I felt I had to see Sylvie again, the only figure alive and young enough to bind me to these parts. I set off back to Loisy. It was noon; everybody was still sleeping off the festivities. I decided to kill some time by walking over to Ermenonville, about two and a half miles away by the forest road. It was perfect summer weather. The coolness of the road, which seemed more like a park lane, delighted me as I set forth. The uniform green of the great oak trees was only relieved by the white trunks of the birches with their quivering leaves. The birds were silent; all I heard was the sound the woodpecker makes as it taps the trees to hollow out its nest. For a moment, I nearly lost my way, for at various points the signposts indicating the different routes display nothing but effaced letters. Finally, leaving the *Desert* to my left, I arrived at the dancing-ring where the bench reserved for the elders can still be seen. All the memories of classical philosophy, revived by the former proprietor of this estate, came rushing back to me at the sight of this picturesque illustration of *Anarcharsis* and *Émile*.[13]

When I saw the glitter of the lake through the branches of the willows and hazels, I recognized it as a spot to which my uncle had often taken me in the course of his walks: it was the *Temple of Philosophy*, an edifice which its founder had not been fortunate enough to complete. Its form is that of the temple of the Tiburtine sibyl[14] and, still standing in the shelter of a clump of pines, it displays the names of all the great thinkers from Montaigne and Descartes to Rousseau. This unfinished structure is now no more than a ruin gracefully entwined with ivy, its steps loosened by the invading bramble. As a young child,

13 Two pedagogical classics of the eighteenth century – Rousseau's *Émile* and Barthélemy's *Voyage de jeune Anacharsis en Grèce*.
14 Nerval had visited the celebrated temple of the Sibyl in Tivoli (Tibur) during his travels in Italy.

it was here that I had witnessed ceremonies at which young girls clad in white were awarded prizes for academic excellence and good conduct. Where are the rose-bushes which once surrounded the hill? The eglantine and raspberry hide the last of them, now reverting to the wild. As for the laurels, have they all been cut? – to quote the song of those lasses who'll to the woods no more. No, these shrubs from fair Italy have simply perished under our misty skies. Fortunately, Virgil's privet still flourishes, as if to underscore the words of the master inscribed above the portal: *Rerum cognoscere causas!*[15] Yes, this temple is crumbling like so many others, and man, weary or forgetful, will turn away from its threshold while nature, indifferent to all, reclaims the terrain that art tried to wrest from her; but the thirst for knowledge will live on forever, the spur of all vitality and all action!

Here is the isle of poplars with Rousseau's tomb, empty of his ashes. O sage! You bestowed the milk of the strong upon us, yet we were too weak to benefit from it. We have forgotten those lessons which you taught our fathers, and we have mislaid

15 *Georgics* II, 490: 'to know the causes of things'.

the meaning of your words, the last echo of ancient wisdom. But let us not despair, let us do as you did at your dying moment and turn our eyes to the sun!

I saw the castle again, the calm waters of its moat, the cascade whispering among the rocks, the roadway linking the two parts of the village, their corners marked by four dovecotes and the great lawn stretching out like a savanna overlooked by shady slopes; in the distance, Gabrielle's tower is reflected in an artificial lake starred with dayflowers; the water foams, the insects hum . . . The air it exhales is treacherous, so we had better beat a retreat to the dusty sandstone of the Desert and the heaths where the green of the ferns is dabbed by touches of pink broom. How sad and lonely all this is! The enchanting look in Sylvie's eyes, the way she scampered about, her cries of joy – how they all used to impart such charm to the scenes I have just been wandering through! She was still a wild little creature then, her feet bare, her skin tanned despite the straw hat she wore with its long ribbon floating carelessly amid the tresses of her black hair. We would go and have milk at the Swiss farm, and they would say to me: 'What a pretty sweetheart you have there, little Parisian.' Ah! In those days no peasant would have danced with her! I

was the only one she danced with, once a year, at the
Festival of the Bow.

x. *Big Curly*

I made my way back to Loisy; everybody was now
awake. Sylvie was dressed like a fine young lady,
almost citified. She invited me up to her room, as
ingenuous as ever. Her eyes still sparkled with a
charming smile, but the pronounced arc of her eyebrows gave her a more serious air at moments. Her
room was simply decorated, although the furnishings
were modern; a gilt-framed mirror had replaced the
old pier glass with its idyllic shepherd offering a nest
to a shepherdess all pink and blue. The four-poster
bed, chastely draped with sprigged chintz, had been
replaced by a walnut affair hung with a curtain
drawn by a rod; at the window, in the cage that
once contained linnets, there were canaries. I was
anxious to leave this room; it contained nothing of
the past. 'You're not working at your lace today?' I
asked Sylvie.

'Oh, I don't make lace any more; there's no more
demand for it; they've even closed the factory at
Chantilly.'

'What do you do, then?' She went over to a corner of the room and brought back an iron instrument that looked like a long pair of pliers. 'What on earth is that?'

'It's what they call an apparatus; it's for holding the leather of gloves so you can sew them.'

'Oh, so you're a glove-maker now, Sylvie?'

'Yes, we take in work for Dammartin; business is good for the moment; but I'm not doing anything today; we can go wherever you want.' I tossed a glance in the direction of Othys: she shook her head; I gathered her aunt was no longer alive. Sylvie called over a young boy and had him saddle up a donkey.

'I'm still worn out from yesterday,' she said, 'but an outing will do me good; let's go to Châalis.' And so there we were, crossing the forest, followed by a little boy holding a switch. After a short while, Sylvie no longer wanted to continue further, and I gave her a kiss as I helped her sit down. Conversation between us could no longer be very intimate. She wanted to hear about my life in Paris, about my travels . . . 'How can anyone travel so far?' she said.

'Seeing you again like this, I'm rather amazed myself.'

'Oh, you're just saying that!'

'You must admit you were never as pretty back then.'

'I wouldn't know.'

'Do you remember back when we were children and you were taller than I?'

'And you were better behaved!'

'Oh, Sylvie!'

'They used to sit each one of us in a pannier and take us on donkey rides.'

'And we never used the formal "you" . . . Do you remember teaching me how to catch crayfish under the bridges of the Thève and Nonette?'

'And do you remember your milk-brother who one day pulled you out of the *waader*?'

'You mean *Big Curly*? He's the one who told me we could wade across . . . the *waader*.'

I quickly shifted the conversation. This memory had vividly reminded me of the period when I used to come to visit these parts, dressed, much to the merriment of the locals, in a small suit of English cut. Only Sylvie thought me well turned out; but I did not dare remind her of the high opinion she had held of me so long ago. I don't know why, but my thoughts wandered to the wedding outfits we had put on at her old aunt's house in Othys. I asked what had become of them. 'Well,' said Sylvie, 'my good aunt lent me her gown to go dancing at the Dammartin carnival, it must have been two years ago. She died the following year, poor thing!'

She was sighing and weeping, so I did not have the heart to ask her how she had happened to end up at a masked ball; but I realized well enough that thanks to her skills as a working woman, Sylvie was no longer a peasant girl. Only her relatives had remained in their station; she lived among them like an industrious fairy, scattering abundance all about her.

XI. *Return*

The view opened up as we emerged from the woods. We had arrived at the banks of the Châalis lakes. The arcades of the cloister, the chapel with its slender ogees, the feudal tower, and the little castle that had housed the loves of Henri IV and Gabrielle[16] were tinged dusk red against the dark green of the woods. 'A landscape straight out of Walter Scott,' Sylvie was saying.

16 Gabrielle d'Estrées, one of the mistresses of Henry IV (1553–1610), husband of Margaret of Valois.

'And who on earth told you about Walter Scott?'
I said. 'You've certainly done a lot of reading these
past three years! . . . As for me, I'm trying to forget
all about books; what delights me is to be with
you, revisiting this ancient abbey where we used
to hide in the ruins as small children. Do you
remember how frightened you were, Sylvie, when
the keeper told us the story about the Red
Monks?'

'Oh, don't remind me!'

'Well, then sing me the song about the fair maiden
who was carried off from her father's garden beneath
the white rose tree.'

'No one sings that one any more.'

'So you're a musician now, are you?'

'Somewhat.'

'Sylvie, Sylvie, I bet you sing opera tunes!'

'So what if I do?'

'Because I used to love those old tunes, and you'll
no longer be able to sing them.'

Sylvie modulated a few bars of a grand aria from
a modern opera . . . She was *phrasing*!

We had strolled past the nearby lakes. Here was
the green lawn surrounded by limes and elms where
we often danced. I was conceited enough to display
my knowledge of the old Carlovingian walls and to

decipher the heraldry of the arms of the House of Este. 'Well,' said Sylvie, 'you've obviously read far more than I have. So you're a man of learning now, are you?'

I was piqued by her tone of reproach. I had been looking around for a suitable location to renew our brief moment of expansiveness that morning; but what could I say to her in the company of a donkey and a very wide-awake small boy who kept wanting to edge up to us just to hear a Parisian talking? I was then unfortunate enough to tell her about the apparition of Châalis still lingering in my mind. I took Sylvie into the very hall of the castle where I had heard Adrienne sing, 'Oh! Let me hear you!' I said to her. 'Let your dear voice resonate through these vaults and chase away the spirit that is tormenting me – be it heaven-sent or straight from hell!' She repeated the words and music after me:

> Angels, descend without delay
> To the depths of purgatory! . . .

'That's a bit gloomy,' she said.

'It's divine . . . Composed, I think, by Porpora[17] and set to a poem translated in the sixteenth century.'

17 Eighteenth-century Neapolitan composer of cantatas.

'I wouldn't know,' Sylvie replied.

We made our way back by the valley, following the road that goes to Charlepont – which the peasants, not naturally inclined to etymology, insist on calling *Châllepont*. Sylvie, tired of riding the donkey, was leaning on my arm. The road was empty; I tried to speak of what was in my heart but, I do not know why, all I could muster were vulgar commonplaces or the occasional overblown phrase from a novel – which Sylvie might well have read. I would then break off into silence in very classical fashion, leaving her somewhat bewildered by my interrupted effusions. When we reached the walls of Saint-S . . ., we had to watch our step. The path lies through marshy fields riddled with small streams. 'Whatever became of the nun?' I blurted out.

'Oh! You and your nun again . . . Well . . . well, as a matter of fact, things ended up rather badly.'

Sylvie wouldn't breathe a word more.

Do women actually sense when words cross one's lips without coming from the heart? One would tend to doubt it, seeing how easily they are deceived and judging from the kinds of choices they most often make: when it comes to love, men are so good at playacting! I've never been very proficient at it myself, even though I know there are women who would gladly agree to be deceived. Besides, there is something sacred to a love that dates back to child-hood. Sylvie, whom I had watched grow up, was like a sister to me. Seducing her was out of the question ... A completely different idea came into my head. At this hour, I said to myself, I would be at the theatre ... I wonder what Aurélie (for that was the name of the actress) is performing tonight? Most likely the role of the princess in that new play. Oh! how moving she is in the third act ... And in that love scene in the second, where she plays against that wrinkled young leading man ...

'A penny for your thoughts!' said Sylvie, and then began to sing:

> At Dammartin there's a-three fair maidens
> And one of them's a-fairer than the day ...

'You little devil!' I exclaimed. 'So you still do know some of the old songs.'

'If you came back here more often, I'd pick them up again,' she said. 'But let's think of practical mat-ters. You have things to attend to in Paris, and I have my work here. We should start heading home: tomorrow I have to be up at daybreak.'

XII. *Old Dodu*

I was about to reply, I was about to throw myself at her feet and offer her my uncle's house – which it was still possible for me to purchase, given that there were several of us in line for the inheritance and that the property had remained undivided – but we were already back at Loisy by now. Dinner was waiting for us. The fine old country smell of onion soup was wafting through the air. Some neighbours had been invited over for this day-after of the festivities. I immediately recognized an ancient woodcutter, Old Dodu, who used to tell us such comic or terrifying tales long into the night. By turns shepherd, messenger, gamekeeper, fisherman and even poacher, Old Dodu whittled cuckoo-clocks and turnspits in his spare time. For many years he had acted as a tour guide in Ermenonville, showing British visitors the spots where Rousseau used to meditate and recounting his final days. It was he who had been the little boy whom the philosopher had employed to keep his herbals in order and whom he instructed to go out and gather the hemlock plants whose juice he extracted and mixed into his *café au lait*.[18] The innkeeper of *The Golden Cross* contested this latter detail, which set off a long-standing feud. People had long been suspicious of a few innocent secrets Old Dodu possessed, such as healing cows with a spell said backwards and making the sign of the cross with his left foot, but he had quickly given up these superstitions – thanks to the memory, he said, of his talks with Jean-Jacques.

'Here you are, little Parisian!' Old Dodu said to me. 'You here to run off with our girls?'

'Me, Old Dodu?'

'You take them into the woods while the wolf's away?'

'Old Dodu, if anybody's the wolf, it's you.'

'Well, I guess I was a wolf as long as I could find myself some lambs, but these days all I ever come across are goats, and they know how to take care of themselves! But you're a wily lot, you Parisians. Jean-Jacques was quite right to say: "Man is corrupted by the poisonous air of cities."'

'Old Dodu, you know only too well that man is corrupted everywhere.'

Old Dodu launched into a drinking song; they all

18 Local Valois legend had it that Rousseau committed suicide in the fashion of Socrates; Nerval at one point considered writing a play or opera on the philosopher's death.

tried in vain to stop him when he came to a certain bawdy stanza that everyone knew by heart. Sylvie refused to sing, despite our entreaties, claiming that singing at the dinner table just wasn't done any more. I had already noticed her sweetheart of yesterday sitting to her left. There was something about his round face and scraggly hair that seemed vaguely familiar. He got up and came over behind my chair, saying: 'So you don't recognize me, you Parisian?' A kindly woman who had joined us for dessert after having served us dinner whispered into my ear: 'Don't you recognize your own milk-brother?' Without her prompting, I would have looked quite foolish.

'Ah, it's you, Big Curly,' I said. 'It's you, the fellow who pulled me out of the *waader*.' Sylvie was laughing heartily at this recognition scene.

'Not to mention,' he said as he kissed me, 'that you had a fine silver watch and that on the way back home you were far more worried about your watch than about yourself, because it had stopped working. You kept saying, "The *beast* is *drownded*, it no longer goes tick-tock; what will my uncle say? . . ."'

'A beast in a watch!' said Old Dodu. 'So this is what they make the children believe in Paris.'

Sylvie was sleepy, I realized I was no longer on

her mind. She went up to her room and, as I embraced her, she said, 'Come and see us tomorrow.'

Old Dodu was still sitting around the table with Sylvain and my milk-brother; we whiled away the evening over a bottle of *ratafiat* from Louvres. 'Men are all equals,' Old Dodu said between snatches of song, 'I'd just as well drink with a pastry-maker as with a prince.'

'Where's the pastry-maker?' I asked.

'Just look right next to you! A young man with ambitions of going into business for himself.'

My milk-brother seemed embarrassed. Now I understood everything. It was my peculiar fate to have a milk-brother in a region associated with Rousseau – who had wanted to abolish wet-nurses. Old Dodu informed me that there was considerable talk of a marriage between Sylvie and Big Curly. I had heard enough. The following day the Nanteuil-le-Haudoin coach took me back to Paris.

XIII. *Aurélie*

To Paris! The trip takes five hours. I was in no hurry to arrive before evening. Around eight o'clock, I was back in my regular box; Aurélie was pouring all her charm and inspiration into some verses feebly inspired by Schiller, the work of a minor talent of the period. She was sublime in the garden scene. During the fourth act, in which she did not appear, I went to buy a bouquet at Madame Prévost's. I slipped an adoring letter in it, signed: *A Stranger*. I said to myself: that should set things in motion for later on – and the following day, I was off to Germany.

What was I going to do there? Try to put my feelings into order. If I were to write a novel, this story of a heart smitten by two simultaneous loves would barely seem credible. It was my own fault that Sylvie was slipping away from me; but seeing her again that day had been enough to elevate my soul: for me she had henceforth taken her place as a smiling statue in the Temple of Wisdom. The gaze in her eyes had held me back from the brink of the abyss. I continued to reject outright the idea of presenting myself to Aurélie in person, of contending with the countless vulgar suitors who rose into her favours for a moment and then fell back crushed. Some day, I said to myself, we shall see if this woman has a heart.

One morning I read in a newspaper that Aurélie was ill. I wrote to her from the mountains of Salzburg.

My letter was so saturated with Germanic mysticism that I could hardly have expected to meet with any success, but then again I wasn't asking for an answer. I was counting somewhat on chance and on – *the unknown.*

Months pass. In the course of my wanderings and idlings, I had undertaken to portray in a poetic action the loves of the painter Colonna for the fair Laura, whom her parents had forced into a nunnery and whom he loved unto his dying day. Something in this subject touched on my own constant preoccupations. The last line of the play written, I had no other desire but to return to France.

What is there now left to tell that is not the story of so many others? I have passed through every circle and every trial of those scenes of ordeal commonly called theatres. 'I have eaten of the drum and drunk of the cymbal,' as the apparently meaningless phrase of the initiates of Eleusis runs. It no doubt means that, if need be, one must pass beyond the bounds of nonsense and absurdity: for me, reason lay in conquering and holding fast to my ideal.

Aurélie had accepted the principal role in the drama I had brought back from Germany. I shall never forget the day she allowed me to read her the play. The love scenes had been written with her in mind. I believe I recited them with spirit, and above all with rapture. In the conversation that ensued, I revealed I was the *Stranger* of the two letters. She said to me: 'You're mad, but come and see me again ... I have yet to find a man who knew how to love me.'

O woman! So it's love you're looking for ... What am I doing then?

During the following days, I wrote her the most tender, most beautiful letters that she had probably ever received. Her replies were full of good sense. At one point, obviously touched, she asked to see me and confessed it would be most difficult for her to break off a previous attachment. 'If you truly love me for *what I am*,' she said, 'you will understand that I cannot belong to more than one man.'

Two months later I received an effusive letter from her. I hastened to her side. Someone had in the meantime informed me of a precious bit of news. The handsome young fellow whom I had seen at the club one night had just enlisted in the Spahis.[19]

The following summer there were horse races at Chantilly. The theatre troupe to which she belonged

19 Algerian cavalry units in the French army.

was giving a performance there. Once in the area, the troupe was at the disposal of its manager for three days. I had become friends with this excellent fellow who had played Dorante in Marivaux's comedies in the distant past and had since been performing the role of the young leading man in various dramas. His latest success had been the part of the lover in the play taken from Schiller where I had seen him so wrinkled through my opera-glasses. Off stage, he seemed younger than his years and, having kept trim, he still could produce an effect in the provinces. He had fire. I was accompanying the troupe in my capacity as *gentleman poet*; I persuaded the manager to give some performances at Senlis and Dammartin. He was more inclined to play Compiègne, but Aurélie sided with me. The following day, while negotiations were going on with the local authorities and the owners of the halls, I rented some horses and we set off along the road that passes by the ponds of Commelle to go and have lunch at the castle of Queen Blanche. Aurélie, dressed in her riding-habit, her blonde hair streaming behind her, rode through the forest like a queen out of another era, and the peasants stopped in amazement. Madame de F . . . was the only other person they had ever seen dispense greetings with such command and grace. After lunch, we visited some villages that recall Switzerland, their sawmills powered by the waters of the Nonette. These scenes, so dear to my memories, interested her, but nothing more. I had planned to take Aurélie to the castle near Orry and show her the great green lawn where I had seen Adrienne for the very first time. She displayed no trace of emotion. Then I told her everything; I told her of the source of this love first glimpsed in the night, then in dreams, and now realized in her. She listened attentively, then said: 'You do not love me! You're expecting me to say: "The actress and nun are one and the same." You're chasing after some drama, that's all, and you can't come up with the dénouement. What nonsense! I no longer believe you at all!'

These words came as an illumination. These bizarre raptures to which I had so long been prey, these dreams, these tears, these fits of despair and tenderness ... so all this was not love? If so, then where is it?

That evening Aurélie performed at Senlis. I seemed to notice that she had a weak spot for the director – the wrinkled young leading man. He was a man of excellent character who had done a great deal for her.

One day Aurélie said to me: 'You know who truly loves me? That man there.'

XIV. *Last Leaf*

Such are the chimeras that beguile and misguide us in the morning of life. I have tried to set them down without much order, but many hearts will understand me. Illusions fall away one after another like the husks of a fruit, and that fruit is experience. It is bitter to the taste, but there is fortitude to be found in gall – forgive me my old-fashioned turns of phrase. Rousseau said the spectacle of nature provides consolation for everything. Sometimes I go looking for my groves of Clarens again, lost somewhere to the north of Paris in the mists. Everything has so changed!

Ermenonville! Land where idylls of antiquity still flourished – retranslated anew from Gessner![20] You have lost your one and only star, the one that sparkled for me with a double splendour. Now blue, now pink, like Aldebaran's deceptive radiance, the

20 Eighteenth-century Swiss poet, author of a number of extraordinarily popular *Idylls*.

star was Adrienne or Sylvie — the two halves of a single love. One was the sublime ideal, the other, sweet reality. What are they to me now, your lakes, your shadowy groves, your desert? Othys, Montagny, Loisy, the poor neighbouring villages, Châalis — now being restored — you have retained nothing of this past. Every now and then I feel the urge to revisit these scenes of solitude and reverie. There I sadly rediscover within myself the fleeting traces of an era when naturalness was affected; I occasionally smile when I read certain lines of Roucher[21] that had once seemed so sublime to me chiselled into the granite rocks — or else maxims of benevolence inscribed above a fountain or a grotto dedicated to Pan. The ponds, dug at such expense, are now stagnant expanses, shunned by swans. The times are gone when the hunting parties of the Condé would sweep through these parts with their proud equestriennes, their horns calling to each other from afar, multiplying with every echo. These days there is no direct route to Ermenonville. Sometimes I travel by way of Creil and Senlis, sometimes by Dammartin.

One never gets to Dammartin before evening. I

21 Minor eighteenth-century didactic poet.

stay the night at the *St John's Image*. They usually give me a fairly clean room, hung with old tapestries and a decorative panel above the mirror. In this room I let myself relapse into that taste for bric-à-brac which I gave up long ago. I sleep well in the warmth of the eiderdown, the customary bedding in these parts. In the morning, I open the window framed with vines and roses and am enraptured by the view, a green horizon stretching for twenty-five miles with poplars lined up along it like soldiers. Here and there, a few villages nestle beneath their steep spires constructed, as they say in the region, like pointed bonework. The first village you see is Othys, then Eve, then Ver; you would be able to make out Ermenonville through the woods if it had a spire – but in this Enlightenment locale the church has been quite neglected. Having filled my lungs with the pure air one breathes in these plains, I merrily make my way downstairs and amble over to the pastry shop. 'Hello there, Big Curly!' 'Hello there, little Parisian!' We trade a few friendly childhood punches, then I climb some stairs where the gleeful cries of two children greet my arrival. The Athenian smile of Sylvie brightens her charmed expression. I say to myself: 'This way lay happiness, perhaps; and yet . . .'

Sometimes I call her Lolotte, and she thinks I look somewhat like Werther, minus the pistols, which have gone out of fashion. While Big Curly prepares breakfast, we take the children for a walk among the alleys of limes that ring the ruins of the castle's ancient towers. While the little ones practise shooting their father's arrows into the straw target on the archery range of the Companies of the Bow, we read poetry together or some pages from those short little books no one writes any more.

I forgot to mention that the day that Aurélie played Dammartin with her troupe, I took Sylvie to the performance and asked her if she did not think that the actress looked like someone she once knew.

'Like whom?'

'Do you remember Adrienne?'

She burst out laughing and said: 'What an idea!' Then, as if regretting this remark, she sighed and added: 'Poor Adrienne! She died in the convent of Saint-S . . ., around 1832.'

Sylvie first appeared in *La Revue des Deux Mondes* in 1853.
It was published in the volume *Les Filles du feu* in 1854.